P9-BXV-678

Autumn's
Secret Gift

Autumn's Secret Gift

Elise Allen
and Halle Stanford

illustrated by
Paige Pooler

BLOOMSBURY
NEW YORK   LONDON   NEW DELHI   SYDNEY

We wish to personally thank Mike Moon for his inspiration for this book, and acknowledge the contributions of Fonda Snyder, Lisa Henson, Melissa Segal, Jill Peterson, and Meghan Sheridan.

First published in the United States of America in August 2014
by Bloomsbury Children's Books
www.bloomsbury.com

Bloomsbury is a registered trademark of Bloomsbury Publishing Plc

For information about permission to reproduce selections from this book, write to Permissions, Bloomsbury Children's Books, 1385 Broadway, New York, NY 10018
Bloomsbury books may be purchased for business or promotional use. For information on bulk purchases please contact Macmillan Corporate and Premium Sales Department at specialmarkets@macmillan.com

Library of Congress Cataloging-in-Publication Data
Allen, Elise, author.
Autumn's secret gift / by Elise Allen and Halle Stanford ; illustrated by Paige Pooler.
    pages   cm   — (Jim Henson's Enchanted sisters)
Summary: Sisters Autumn, Winter, Spring, and Summer are nature's royalty. In Mother Nature's realm, they're responsible for each magical turn of the seasons. When Autumn loses a special gift from Mother Nature, can the sisters find the gift before Mother Nature's party?
    ISBN 978-1-61963-254-7 (paperback) • ISBN 978-1-61963-256-1 (hardcover)
                        ISBN 978-1-61963-255-4 (e-book)
[1. Seasons—Fiction. 2. Nature—Fiction. 3. Magic—Fiction. 4. Sisters—Fiction.
5. Friendship—Fiction. 6. Lost and found possessions—Fiction.] I. Stanford, Halle, author.
                    II. Pooler, Paige, illustrator. III. Title.
        PZ7.A42558Au 2014   [Fic]—dc23   2013048654

Book design by John Candell
Printed and bound in the U.S.A. by Thomson-Shore Inc., Dexter, Michigan
                2 4 6 8 10 9 7 5 3 1 (paperback)
                2 4 6 8 10 9 7 5 3 1 (hardcover)

All papers used by Bloomsbury Publishing, Inc., are natural, recyclable products made from wood grown in well-managed forests. The manufacturing processes conform to the environmental regulations of the country of origin.

CHAPTER
1

Is there anything better than riding on an elephant with your three best friends in the world?

No, Autumn thought, *there is not.*

She and her Sparkle Sisters, Spring, Winter, and Summer, rode together in a padded carriage that rested on the elephant's back. The elephant was named Whisper, and he was Autumn's pet. The carriage was covered with a canopy, but the sides were open to let in the crisp fall breeze. The air smelled like fresh apples and falling leaves. Autumn and her sisters sipped from mugs of cider and nibbled at the pumpkin muffins they balanced on their laps.

Perfection.

Autumn glanced at her long glittering scepter, propped next to her against the seat. Each of the

Sparkles had a scepter, and each wore a glistening headband with a gem right in the center. The gems sparkled with the same colors as the orbs on top of their scepters. At least, most of the time they were the same colors. Right now Autumn noticed that each of their orbs was almost covered in a silver mist. Only a thin crescent of color peeked through, yet even as she watched, that bright part grew smaller, swallowed by the silver.

Very soon she and her sisters would have to leave and perform the Sparkle Ceremony that would turn summer to autumn for the Outworlders, or "humans," as Mother Nature called them. The Outworlders were from a realm just a step outside their own, and they had no idea the Sparkles even existed. Winter said she didn't think that was fair at all. She said the Sparkles worked so hard to change the seasons, there should be Sparkle Sister statues in every Outworlder city!

Autumn understood how Winter felt, but she didn't agree. She didn't need statues to help others. In fact, she thought it was even more special that the

Sparkles' season-changing powers were a beautiful secret. Besides, changing the seasons wasn't just their Sparkle Sister duty, it was their joy. The Sparkle Ceremony wasn't always easy, but working together to accomplish it was the best feeling in the world.

At the moment, though, Autumn was perfectly happy just to sit back and relax with her sisters. "In two hundred years," she said with a sigh, "I'm going to remember this as one of the happiest days of my life."

Winter laughed so hard she snorted her cider, which made Summer burst out laughing too.

"Why are you laughing?" Autumn asked. "It's true!"

"We know." Spring giggled. "But you *always* say that!"

"Every day!" Winter agreed now that she'd caught her breath. "So in two hundred years, you're going to have *two hundred years'* worth of happiest days of your life. It will take you another two hundred years just to remember them all!"

"Then I have *four* hundred very happy years

ahead of me," Autumn said. She reached out to hold hands with her sisters so they formed a circle. Winter lasted exactly one minute before she leaped to her feet, swaying a little to keep her balance on Whisper's rocking back. "Let's play a game!" she cried.

"You'll give us three guesses, and the first two don't count?" Summer asked.

"I'll give you three guesses, and the first two don't—" Winter scrunched her face as she realized what Summer had said. "Okay, so you already know: Sparkle-Dare."

Winter fixed her eyes on Autumn, but it was Spring who responded. Her tinkle-bell giggle danced on the breeze as she said, "Autumn doesn't play Sparkle-Dare. You know that."

"*I* do, though," Summer said, getting to her feet. It was tough to say who was more adventurous, Summer or Winter, but the two always had fun trying to win the title. "What do you think? Sparkle-Dare me to jump onto that apple tree?"

She pointed up ahead. Whisper had brought

them into Autumn's apple orchard, which burst with fruit trees and giant oval bales of fresh hay. The tree Summer chose was one of the largest. It would take a huge leap to vault onto one of its branches. Spring's always-wide violet eyes grew even larger.

"Don't do it!" she cried, clutching at Summer's gauzy green dress.

"Spring, it's fine," Summer assured her. "I've done it a million times."

"Which is why I want *Autumn* to do something," Winter said. "It can even be something easy, like . . . slide down Whisper's back and into a hay pile."

"I love it!" exclaimed Summer. "I go after Autumn!"

"But I'm not going," Autumn said. "Why would I jump out of a perfectly good carriage?"

"Because it's *fun!*" Winter insisted.

Autumn took a long sip of her cider, closing her eyes so she could better taste its cinnamony sweetness. When she opened them again, Winter had moved so close that her face was mere inches away. The fur on her hood tickled Autumn's cheeks.

"Pleeeeeeease?" Winter begged.

"Another day," Autumn promised. "When I know in advance. Then I'll be ready."

"But that's the point!" Winter said. "You always think and plan everything out. Just once, I want to see you do something completely out of the blue. Just *once*!"

"I do things out of the blue." Autumn was ready to shoot back an example … but she couldn't. Not one thing came to mind. Was that really possible? Had she *never* done anything without planning it first?

"Oh!" Spring squealed, holding up her scepter. "We have to go!"

All the sisters turned to look. The orb on Spring's purple scepter now showed only a thin line of color uncovered by silver mist.

It was time. They each pulled out their scepters and touched the four orbs together as they recited:

"Rainbow come and take us fast,
The season's turn is here at last!"

Each Sparkle touched her scepter orb to the gem on her headband. Glittering rainbow light soared upward, making a pathway to the sky. The Sparkles raised their scepters into the middle of the rainbow and were pulled off their feet and right through the top of Whisper's carriage. They didn't even feel it; when they rode the rainbow, they were part of its magical light, not held back by anything.

Spring giggled. She always giggled when she traveled by rainbow, no matter how often she did it. She'd told Autumn she loved the feathery feeling in the pit of her stomach, as if she'd swallowed a baby bird and it was dancing around inside her.

Summer whooped with delight and turned somersaults. She always said that if she had her way she'd fly all the time, not just when she was traveling to Mother Nature or one of her sisters' realms.

Autumn didn't make a sound. She took the rainbow ride very seriously. To her it was majestic and special. She closed her eyes and felt the ripples of warmth wash over her face. If she concentrated hard enough, she was sure she could feel seven slightly different textures of warmth, one for each bar of glittering color.

Next to her, Autumn heard Winter shout, "Summer, try this!" and felt the rush of air that meant her daredevil sisters were playing with new tricks as they soared through the sky. They screamed and laughed so hard that Autumn couldn't help smiling too. Maybe one day she'd try to play in the rainbow like them. She'd just have to plan it first. That way she'd be sure nothing would go wrong.

Plan it first . . . Isn't that what Winter said she *always* did?

An uncomfortable prickle ran over her skin, but she shook it off. So she liked to plan. What was wrong with that?

Autumn's head went swimmy with the weightless feeling that meant they'd reached the very top of the rainbow arc. As always, she snapped open her eyes, eager to see this incredible view of their world. It was laid out in a circle, divided into four Seasonal Sparkledoms. You could tell just by the colors which Sparkledom was which. Spring's bloomed with flowering pinks, purples, and greens. Winter's world glistened with icy white and blue. Summer's realm radiated sandy yellows and fields of green. Autumn's own land glowed with dappled oranges and reds.

In the center of everything was Mother Nature's realm, the perfect blend of all the seasonal colors. Just looking at it, Autumn felt warm all over, as if Mother were giving her a huge hug.

Autumn let her eyes stray to the outskirts of the Sparkledoms. She shuddered. Beyond the four sisters' realms was a sprawling wilderness of dry, lifeless thorns, crags, and brush. There was no sparkle in that place. Dark clouds hid much of the land, but flashes of angry lightning showed skeletal tree limbs and charred earth. Autumn could see the spirals of ten tornadoes, and gasped as an earthquake split the ground into a wide canyon.

This terrible land was the Barrens. It belonged to Bluster Tempest and his Weeds: Sleet, Thunderbolt, Twister, and Quake. The Barrens was an awful place, but it was separated from the Sparkledoms by an invisible barrier. If they wanted to, the Sparkles could easily walk through the barrier, but they never did. There was no reason to visit Bluster and the Weeds, who loved chaos and disorder, and always tried to interfere with the Sparkle Ceremony. The sisters had to be careful all the time. If anything got in the way of the Ceremony and the girls couldn't complete it properly, it would mean disaster for the Outworlders.

Sometimes Autumn wished Mother Nature

would use her powers to send Bluster and the Weeds away forever, but then she remembered Mother's words. Sleet, thunderbolts, twisters, and quakes were part of nature, she had said. Bluster and the Weeds balanced Mother and the Sparkles in an important way. The world needed them all.

Autumn closed her eyes again for the ride down the rainbow. The wind whipped her long black braid behind her, and she reached out with all her senses to feel when she was close to the ground. At just the right moment she stepped gently out of the glowing rainbow light. Her slippered feet crunched onto the grass.

This was always her favorite moment—that first second after she arrived in Mother Nature's Sparkle-dom. She kept her eyes closed and breathed in as deeply as she could to take in its unique aroma. It was the smell of every season mixed together, combinations found nowhere else. Autumn smelled the ocean and newly mown grass, an orange grove and a crackling bonfire, snowy pine trees and sunflowers.

She drank it all in until she felt something tickle her chin. She gasped and her eyes snapped open, bringing her face-to- ... well ... sort-of-face with a very startled vine. The vine stood as tall as Autumn, its tip crooked forward like a pointed bird head.

That alone didn't shock Autumn. In Mother Nature's Sparkledom, every living thing had a mind of its own and could move freely, even the plants. The problem wasn't that the vine was alive, but that it snuck up on her.

"You startled me!" she scolded.

The plant reared back and quickly darted behind Mother Nature, who laughed kindly.

"It's okay, little one," she comforted the still-shaking vine.

Mother's voice was a cozy blanket bundling Autumn tight. Mother had that effect on all the girls. On the plants too, judging from the way the frightened vine relaxed onto Mother's shoulder. None of the Sparkles knew how old Mother was, though they guessed she was at least a bazill-atill-ajillion. She didn't look it. She stood tall and strong, with a huge burst of dark curls crowning her ebony skin. Mother Nature could outrun a cheetah, arm wrestle a gorilla, and then cradle the most delicate baby bird. The whole world adored her. Plants and animals were drawn to her like she was a sun, and she spoke the language of every living thing.

If you asked the Sparkles, they'd tell you everything good in the universe was wrapped up in Mother Nature. They would do anything to please her, and even though she would never do more than say she was disappointed if they messed up, none of the girls could think of anything worse.

"I'm sorry, Autumn," Mother said, still cuddling the vine. "This little plant forgot how much you dislike being surprised. He says he'd like to make it up to you."

The vine nodded its tip, then leaped off Mother's

shoulder and stood perfectly straight . . . before twirling and flailing in the most ridiculous dance Autumn had ever seen. Everyone laughed and applauded.

Winter leaned in close to Autumn. "See?" she said. "Even Mother knows you need everything all planned out."

Autumn was hurt. Her face must have shown it, because Winter quickly added, "I'm just saying, it's okay to let go and have fun."

Before Autumn could respond, a loud coo trilled through the air. She looked up and saw a large sparkling blue dove. It soared down from the sky and landed on Mother's shoulder. This was Serenity, whose always-peaceful nature perfectly matched her name. She was Mother's top advisor, and Mother listened carefully as the dove cocked her head toward Mother's ear and cooed again. Mother nodded, then held out her scepter, as silver as Autumn's own.

"It's time to go to Evergrass Circle!" Mother called. "The Sparkle Ceremony is about to begin!"

CHAPTER
2

Autumn snaked her body to the beat, each step practiced and perfect. *Hip-swing, arm-swing, deep squat and twirl—*

"Ow!"

She winced as her ankle turned. Summer looked over midleap to raise a concerned eyebrow, but Autumn kept dancing, barely missing a beat.

This wasn't like Autumn. She rarely let her emotions run away with her, and she certainly wouldn't lose control during a Sparkle Ceremony. And not just any Sparkle Ceremony. Today would bring *her* season to the Outworlders. It was her most important day of the year. She could *not* make any more mistakes.

She thudded down on Winter's foot.

Oops.

Okay, maybe just that *one* more.

"Ouch!" Winter cried. "You okay?"

"I'm fine," Autumn whispered back. "Sorry."

She twirled away, determined to pull it together.

This was all Winter's fault. Why did she say that about Mother? It was one thing if Winter didn't like Autumn planning so much, but if Mother felt the same way...Autumn felt sick just thinking about it.

That was silly though. Mother didn't say she had a problem with Autumn. She just pointed out that Autumn didn't like to be surprised...which she didn't! It was only Winter who made it sound like that was a bad thing.

Autumn stumbled over a pivot step and landed flat on her bottom. Mother didn't see. Spring did, though, and her jaw dropped lower than her plié. Autumn scrambled back to her feet.

This was bad. Any more mistakes and she risked wrecking the whole Sparkle Ceremony, plunging the Outworlders into an endless summer. Without the relief of autumn, their world would grow so blazingly hot that everything would burn to a crisp.

Autumn only knew one way to bring back her focus. Keeping the beat of the dance, she touched her middle fingers to her thumbs, and took a deep breath. While her body moved, she forced her mind to concentrate on every detail she could see. She marveled at the perfectly round patch of shimmering green lawn at her feet. She thrilled to Evergrass Circle's border of lush trees, so tall they blocked all but the beautiful blue disk of sky above them. Autumn knew the Outworlders shared this bit of sky, and that connection made the area buzz with powerful energy. That energy grew as the Sparkles danced around Mother Nature, and the power of the Sparkle Ceremony rushed between them.

Autumn wasn't distracted anymore. She only felt this moment, as every bit of joy inside her flowed into her dance. A huge grin spread across her face as the trees, flowers, and grass began to sing in voiceless rhythms: rustling leaves, branches rat-a-tatting together, wind whistling through tall grasses. It all grew louder and faster, and Autumn didn't know if she was moving to the plants' beat or they were moving to hers. She leaped, clapped, and twirled until everything in her body told her *this* was the moment. With a mighty cry, she lunged forward, both hands holding her scepter high.

"We make the call, turn summer to fall!" she shouted.

Her sisters echoed her call and her motion as Mother Nature raised her own scepter into the air. A bolt of colored light leaped from each Sparkle's headband gem to the orbs on their scepters, which shuddered with growing power until Autumn was afraid she couldn't hold on a second longer. Suddenly, the sparkling whirls of light in her and her sisters' scepters bolted across the lawn and into Mother Nature's own orb. The four beams converged in a glow so bright that Autumn shut her eyes. When she looked again, the dazzling lights were swirling into a tumble of orange, yellow, blue, and violet that shrank into smaller and smaller circles until they disappeared.

To a stranger, this might look like the end. Autumn and her sisters knew better. While Mother Nature stood absolutely still, the four of them exchanged glances and tried to contain their smiles until Winter counted down in a low whisper, "...three, two, one..."

A volcano erupted from the gem on Mother Nature's headband. Brilliant shooting-star sparkles streamed upward in a column that stretched as far as the eye could see, though the sisters knew it went even farther. This was their supercharged Sparkle Power, and it pulsed against the very point where the girls' world met the Outworlders'. From there, the power shimmered across the Outworlders' entire realm, turning the season and keeping nature in balance.

When the last bit of sparkle-geyser left Mother's gem and hit the sky, it burst into red, yellow, and orange leaf-shaped fireworks. The display was always in shapes and colors to honor the brand-new season, and marked the end of a successful Sparkle Ceremony. Autumn heard her sisters cheer, but she was

too happy to shout. She just smiled and held her feelings close.

As always at this moment, Autumn thought about the Outworlders. They knew nothing about the Sparkle Ceremony, but Mother said they could see the fireworks; the display looked different to them. Mother said they called it the "northern lights," and while they shone brightest on Ceremony days, Mother said that in just the right spots, their echoes

could be seen dancing in the sky even between Cere-
monies. Autumn imagined an Outworlder looking up
at those lights at this very moment, just like Autumn
herself. She felt a connection to that Outworlder
whom she'd never know, and it filled her heart.

"Well done, my girls!"

Mother Nature's voice drew Autumn's attention
away from the sky, and she and her sisters rushed to
Mother for a group hug. Afterward, the Sparkles
raised their scepters to the sky, ready to ride back
home, but Mother stopped them.

"Autumn, can you stay a moment?"

Autumn froze. Mother always liked to rest by
herself after the Ceremony. Why would she want
Autumn to stay? Had Mother realized she'd almost
ruined the Ceremony? Was Mother upset? Autumn
checked with her sisters. Summer stood straighter,
as if she sensed danger. Winter gave a low whistle. Spring nervously bit her bottom lip. Autumn
could tell they felt bad for her, so she tried to be
brave.

"Of course," she said.

Mother nodded to the other Sparkles, gently dismissing them. Reluctantly, the three raised their scepters in the air and chanted together:

"Rainbow come and don't be slow,
The season's changed, so home we go!"

They touched their scepters to the gems in their headbands, and Autumn watched as three sparkly rainbows streamed out to carry her sisters back home. Autumn kept watching even after her sisters left and the shimmery lights disappeared. Better to look there than at Mother and see the disappointed look on her face. Autumn's insides twisted as she pictured it.

Yet when she did look up, Mother was smiling down at her.

"I messed up the Sparkle Ceremony," Autumn blurted. "I almost ruined everything. I feel terrible."

"We can't have that." Mother clucked. She waved her scepter, and a patch of giant pumpkins sprouted from the ground, each carved with a jack-o'-lantern face so silly it made Autumn laugh out loud. The jack-o'-lanterns joined in, giggling and chuckling right along with her.

"That's what I want to hear," Mother said. "Happiness!"

"But I—" Autumn protested.

"You got lost in your own head," Mother said. "I have no doubt it's a fascinating place to wander. But I was never worried. I knew in the end you'd come through."

"I knew it too," boomed a deep-voiced jack-o'-lantern.

"You did not!" another retorted.

"I knew it before all of you," a long, skinny jack-o'-lantern claimed.

"You weren't even there!" piped another.

Soon the entire patch of jack-o'-lanterns was squabbling so loudly that Autumn couldn't make out any words, just a jumble of screeches and shouts.

"Enough!" Mother said. She waved her scepter and all the jack-o'-lanterns' mouths disappeared. Another wave and two vines sprouted from the ground and wove themselves into a low bench. Mother Nature sat, then gestured for Autumn to join her. Once she did, Mother said, "But if you have something on your mind and want to talk about it, I'm here."

Autumn was too embarrassed to admit what had really bothered her. Instead she said, "It's nothing. I'm okay."

The look in Mother's eyes made Autumn feel like her mother already knew every little thing going on in Autumn's mind. Then Mother smiled.

"Excellent," she said. "Because there's a reason I asked you to stay. I have a favor to ask, and you are perfect for the job."

Autumn sat up straighter. "Me?"

"Yes," Mother said. "It's a matter that requires great responsibility." She looked up, as if searching for spies, then turned a raised-eyebrow gaze on the mouthless jack-o'-lanterns. "Can I trust you all to behave?"

The jack-o'-lanterns nodded. Mother waved her scepter, and their mouths reappeared. "You know what to do," Mother told them. "Let me know if you see her."

"Aye, aye!" the jack-o'-lanterns chorused.

"See who?" Autumn asked.

Mother placed a finger over her lips, then waved her scepter again. A new pumpkin sprouted from the ground, this one huge and hollow. It grew around Mother and Autumn, enclosing them inside. Autumn couldn't see anything until another scepter wave from Mother filled the space with glittering lightning bugs. Their glows reflected off the inside of the pumpkin and cast everything in an orange shine.

"Serenity," Mother answered Autumn's question. "As you know, today is her birthday."

Autumn nodded. She did know. Mother had invited the sisters to a party at sundown in Mother's Sparkledom to celebrate.

"But did you know," Mother asked, "that in all Serenity's life, no matter how hard I tried, I have never once managed to surprise her?"

"Never?"

"Not once," Mother answered. "Until this year."

She winked and waved her scepter once more. The bottom of their pumpkin bubbled as a walnut-shaped seed pod rose out of the ground. Mother pulled it open like a treasure chest and gently took out the most delicate blanket Autumn had ever seen. It was woven from petals, leaves, and needles in every color. It was so thin it was almost see-through, and it twinkled like the stars.

"It's beautiful." Autumn sighed.

"I'm awfully proud of it," Mother admitted. "It's made with spiderweb silk. That's what keeps it strong. Feel it."

She slung the blanket over Autumn's shoulders. It was so cozy-warm she wanted to melt into it. "It's perfect," Autumn said. "Serenity will love it."

"I hope so," Mother said. "But it's very important to me that she doesn't see it before it's time. Can you keep it safe in your kingdom and bring it to the party tonight?"

Autumn couldn't believe her ears. Out of all the Sparkles, out of everyone in their entire world, Mother wanted *her* to hold on to Serenity's present?

"I would be honored," she said.

"Serenity alert!" a jack-o'-lantern cried. "On the horizon, eleven o'clock!"

"Not eleven o'clock," another jack-o'-lantern snapped. "She's at five o'clock!"

"Five o'clock from where you sit," the first jack-o'-lantern boomed. "From here it's eleven!"

"I have half past ten," another jack-o'-lantern said.

"We mean the direction, not the actual time, pumpkin head!"

"Hey! Who are you calling pumpkin head, gourd-face?"

Mother laughed. "You should go," she told Autumn. "Thank you."

"You're welcome," Autumn said. She quickly tucked the precious blanket into the folds of her dress, then raised her scepter in the air as she chanted:

"Rainbow come and take me home,
The time has come to end this roam!"

She touched her scepter to the orange gem in her headband, and as the sparkling rainbow streamed out to carry her back home, she tingled with excitement. Nothing would get in the way of her safely delivering Serenity's blanket tonight.

Nothing.

CHAPTER
3

The second Autumn stepped out of the glittering rainbow light into her own realm, her sisters surrounded her.

"What did Mother say?"

"Is everything all right?"

"Did you get in trouble?"

Even Whisper was worried. The elephant curled his trunk around Autumn in a tight hug.

A little too tight. Autumn could barely breathe. She looked to Summer for help.

"Let's back up and give her space," Summer said. "You too, Whisper."

Autumn gasped as Whisper relaxed his trunk. He kept it draped gently over her shoulder, where Autumn could scratch the orange, leaf-patterned skin.

"So tell us," Summer asked, "are you okay?"

"I'm fine," Autumn promised. "Everything is fine."

"Mother wasn't . . . disappointed?" Spring's violet eyes welled up at even the mention of the terrible word. Autumn took her hands to comfort her.

"Not at all!"

"'Concerned' then, right?" Winter asked. "If it's not 'disappointed,' it's 'concerned.' Just as awful."

"No, no, it wasn't like that," Autumn said. "She knew I messed up, but she wasn't upset."

"Then . . . why'd she keep you back?" Winter asked.

Autumn didn't know what to say. She was dying to share what happened, but she didn't want to hurt her sisters' feelings. What if they got jealous that Mother chose *her* to watch Serenity's gift and not them?

"It was something good," Summer said. "Your smile is even wider than your face."

"Yes, it was," Autumn admitted. She tried to leave it there, but she couldn't stop grinning, and she thought she might burst if she didn't tell them everything. Still, she wasn't positive it was the right thing to do.

As always, Summer seemed to understand.

"It's okay," she said. "You don't have to tell us."

"Yes, you do!" Winter insisted. "I can't take the suspense!"

Autumn laughed. She was probably being overly careful. It's not like Mother *asked* her to keep the blanket a secret from her sisters.

"Okay, that's it," Winter said. "If you don't tell us in two seconds, I'm tickling Spring."

"What?" Spring gasped.

"Oooh, can I help?" Summer asked.

"Summer!" Spring exclaimed.

But Summer and Winter were both grinning now, moving closer and closer to their incredibly ticklish sister.

"Autumn!" Spring pleaded.

"All right!" Autumn cried. "I'll tell you."

Instantly, her sisters dropped everything and turned to face her. Winter plopped to the ground, cross-legged, and rested her chin on her hands. "Yes?"

Carefully, Autumn reached into her pocket and pulled out Mother's blanket. Her sisters gaped.

"It's so twinkly." Spring sighed. "Can I touch it?"

"Of course," Autumn said. "Just be gentle."

Spring ran her hand over the woven petals and leaves. "It's beautiful," she whispered. "You're really lucky to get something so special from Mother."

Spring's eyes clouded over with sadness, and Autumn rushed to explain.

"This isn't a gift for me," she said. "Mother made it for Serenity. For her birthday. She just gave it to me to hold and keep a secret."

Summer nodded. "So it would stay a surprise. She knew you'd keep it safe. That's smart."

Winter snorted. "No smarter than giving it to any of the rest of us."

"That's not true," Spring said. "If she gave it to me, I'd be too afraid I'd lose it. Autumn's perfect."

"Yeah," Winter muttered. *"Perfect."*

Autumn moved to her sister and put her hand on Winter's shoulder. "Please don't be jealous."

"Jealous?" Winter laughed. "I'm not jealous at all! Mother's right. It's like I said this morning—you never do anything without thinking and planning it out. If I had something I wanted to keep safe, I'd give it to you too. That way I'd know nothing would happen to it. Seriously—*nothing* would happen to it."

That sounded mean. Autumn didn't like it. "What are you saying?"

"She's saying you're responsible." Summer jumped

in. She stared at Winter as she said it, as if urging her to agree.

Winter shrugged. "Yeah. You're responsible."

That's what she said, but Autumn knew it wasn't what she meant. Winter thought she was *boring*, and *that's* why Mother Nature could trust her with the blanket. Well, maybe she *was* a little boring, but she'd rather be boring and trustworthy than wild and—

Spring broke into her thoughts with a high-pitched squeal. "I have an idea! How about we all play a game?"

It was an odd moment for such a suggestion, but Autumn knew her sister. Spring couldn't bear to hear any of them fight with one another. She would do anything to make things light and happy again.

"Okay, let's," Autumn agreed. "What should we play?"

"I know," Winter said. "Let's have a Sparkle-Powers Contest!"

Autumn sighed. Winter *always* wanted to have a Sparkle-Powers Contest. Each of the Sparkles had a special power tied to her season. There weren't any rules about how they could use their powers, but Autumn felt like they shouldn't be used without a purpose. Winter, she knew, couldn't disagree more. Their Sparkle Powers were *fun*, Winter always said. And besides, if they wanted to truly master their powers, didn't they need to practice?

"I'm in," Summer said. "Spring?"

"Okay, sure!" Spring chirped. "How about you, Autumn?"

"I'll judge," Autumn said. It was her usual compromise. It meant she could play without using her powers. It also meant she could declare a tie no matter what. She crunched over the fallen leaves and made her way to Whisper, then nickered softly. Whisper lowered his trunk and pushed it against her legs, sweeping her off her feet and swinging her to his back. Autumn started to fold Mother's blanket again, but it was so shimmery she didn't want to take her eyes off it. Instead she spread it out carefully on Whisper's back, and rubbed one soft edge between her thumb and forefinger.

"Okay," she said, "the Sparkle-Powers Contest starts *now*!"

"Me first!" Winter cried. She raced to a pyramid of hay bales and scrambled to the top. She pulled her scepter from the inside pocket of her parka, held it high in the air, and cried:

"Winter's chill is twice as nice,
When all the world is turned to ice!"

She swirled the scepter above her head, then touched it to the hay bale under her feet. Blue sparkles flew out of her scepter and danced over the hay. When the sparkles disappeared, the entire bale was frozen into a giant iceberg. Winter squealed with delight as she threw herself onto her bottom and slid down its side.

Autumn clapped. "Very impressive."

"That was excellent!"

Summer cried. "I want to ride down too!" She scrambled up the mountain of ice, but her sandals didn't have the grip of Winter's boots, and she kept sliding hopelessly back down. "That's it," she finally declared. "I'm changing it up."

She unhooked her own scepter from her belt and aimed it at the ice.

"The summer sun bears no defeat,
Give me all its glow and heat!"

Summer shut her eyes tight as a bolt of the brightest yellow sparkles screamed out of her scepter and covered the mountain of ice. The ice melted instantly into a massive *SPLOOSH* of water that rushed downhill like a river.

"This is more like it!" Summer threw herself onto her stomach and slipped and slid down the hill, laughing all the way. At the bottom, she called up to her sisters. "Now *that* was a ride!"

"But you're all wet!" Spring called down to her.

Actually, Summer was *soaked*. Her long brown hair clung to her face in dripping strings, and her sandals squished with every step she took back up the hill.

"Easily fixed," she said with a smile. She raised her scepter high in the air. It was still so charged from her last burst of magic that she didn't even have to chant. It easily rained warm yellow sparkles down on her. When they faded, she was perfectly dry.

"No fair," Winter said. "You're only supposed to use your Sparkle Powers once in the contest."

"The second time doesn't count," Autumn said from her seat on Whisper. "Spring? Do you want a turn?"

"Sure!" Spring said. "I just need to think..."

She twisted her blond hair around one finger, then slowly turned her whole body in a circle. She spun faster and faster until she collapsed giggling into a pile of fallen leaves.

"Are you okay?" Autumn asked.

"Of course!" Spring said. "Why?"

Her sisters exchanged looks. "Because we were in the middle of a Sparkle-Powers Contest," Winter said. "It's your turn."

"Oh, right!" Spring said. "I forgot! I was twirling

my hair, and that reminded me how much I love twirling around, because my dress swirls out when I spin—see?" She jumped back up to twirl again, and the purple skirt of her dress poofed out like a blooming upside-down tulip. "It keeps going even when I stop."

"Sparkle-Powers Contest?" Winter urged.

"Yes! Okay, I know—here I go." Spring pulled out her scepter and chanted:

"Spring's the happiest time I know,
'Cause everything begins to grow!"

She moved her lips silently as if reciting a wish, then blew a kiss to her scepter orb. Violet sparkles danced out of it like dandelion fluff. They fluttered to the ground, where a patch of fresh green shoots sprouted up. More sprouts burst from the ground in a long path that stopped in front of Whisper. Whisper sniffed curiously at the fresh shoots, then jumped back in alarm as the plants grew taller and larger. They grew right over Whisper's trunk, coating it in shimmering green vines and newly blossomed flowers. When Whisper tugged his trunk away, he broke his connection to Spring's spell, but his trunk remained covered in a tube of green, pink, and purple stripes, woven from the freshly grown blooms.

"It's a Trunk Cozy!" Spring squealed. "Doesn't he look adorable in it?"

Summer, Winter, and Autumn actually thought Whisper looked kind of silly. Whisper himself didn't seem so sure either. He curled his trunk upward to get a better look, then trumpeted his approval. He lumbered to Spring and nuzzled her cheek with his newly cozied trunk.

"He loves it!" Spring giggled.

"Go ahead, Autumn," Summer said. "Tell us the winner."

"Summer, you know she'll say it's a tie," Spring said.

"No, she won't," Winter said. "Autumn, this time I want you to compete too."

"Winter . . . ," Autumn objected.

"Come on, please?" begged Winter. "It'll be so

much more fun if you play too. And think how surprised Mother will be when you tell her you did something different!"

There it was again. Did Winter know something Autumn didn't? Would Mother be happier with her if Autumn tried something a little unexpected?

"I'm in," Autumn said.

But the second the words were out, she felt uncomfortable. She didn't want to do a Powers Contest, but she did want to prove something to Winter...and to Mother. She gave the soft edge of Serenity's blanket a final touch to make sure it was safe, then smoothed it down over Whisper's back. She pulled out her scepter and held it so the orb rested close to her heart. Her Sparkle Power was creating wind, but if she was going to do this contest, she wanted to use her power in just the right way. Something that would give Winter a little nudge for pushing her into this.

She smiled when it came to her. She'd send a light gust right at Winter. Nothing big, just enough to blow Winter's hood off her head. Autumn chanted:

*"Autumn's winds make quite a show,
When through the leaves they start
to blow!"*

Autumn flicked her wrist . . . but something was wrong. Her emotions were all mixed up and wild, and that made her power wild too. The orange sparkles that were supposed to do no more than nudge Winter's hood swirled in the air. They kicked up a massive gust that grew twisted and tumultuous. Leaves slapped at Whisper and the Sparkles as the wind grabbed every red, yellow, and orange leaf from the ground and whipped them in a dizzying kaleidoscope.

Spring wiped leaves from her face. "Fireflies and frights!" she exclaimed. "Please make it stop!"

"I can't!" Autumn wailed. A leaf flew into her mouth, and she plucked it out before adding, "I can only *make* the wind! It always stops on its own!"

"Duck down under Whisper!" Summer cried. "He'll cover us!"

Autumn could barely see through the flying leaves, and her own braid kept smacking her in the cheek, but somehow she managed to slide down Whisper's back and join her sisters. They huddled together under Whisper's belly. As the pelting died down, Autumn felt a sickening chill run up her spine.

"The blanket!" she gasped. She'd left it on Whisper's back! She jumped to her feet to reach for it . . . but it was gone.

"No!" she cried.

Her heart pounding, she dropped to her knees and tore through piles of newly fallen leaves. "Help me!" she called to her sisters . . . but none of them joined her. Instead they all stared at a spot on the horizon. With a sinking feeling in her stomach, Autumn followed their gaze.

Serenity's blanket—the gift Mother had trusted her to protect—was sailing far off into the sky.

CHAPTER
4

All four sisters stood completely still.

"No," Autumn whispered. "This isn't happening."

"I'm so sorry, Autumn." Spring's voice was quiet. She slipped her hand into Autumn's.

"We have to do something," Winter insisted.

"You already did!" Autumn snapped. "You made me do the contest! This is all your fault!"

"It is not!" Winter retorted. "And I didn't *make* you do anything!"

"You guys—stop!" Summer said. "Look!"

She pointed into the sky, where the blanket had floated even farther away. Its rainbow of colors now looked washed out and white, almost like a cloud.

"It's reflecting the snow," Summer said. "It crossed into Winter's Sparkledom."

"So we can still catch up with it?" Spring asked hopefully.

Summer nodded. "If we ride the rainbow." She turned to Autumn. "This is not over. We'll get the blanket back before tonight, and Mother will never know. But we have to work together. Can you do that?"

Autumn glared at Winter, but she was already a lot less angry. She knew it was her own fault the blanket was gone, not Winter's. She felt lucky her sisters wanted to help get it back.

"Yes," she told Summer, "thank you. I would love your help. *All* your help," she added to Winter.

Winter smiled, and all four Sparkles pulled out their scepters, touched the orbs together, and recited:

*"Rainbow arc over cold and snow,
To Winter's home we long to go!"*

They touched their scepter orbs to the gems on their headbands and soared magically through the sparkling rainbow light. This time, however, none of them were turning somersaults or enjoying the view.

"There!" Winter cried as they neared her icy Spar-kledom. Autumn looked where she pointed and saw the blanket. It had landed in a tall evergreen tree, and was almost entirely covered by a fresh dusting of snow. Autumn never would have picked it out with-out Winter's help.

"Daisies and dragonflies, we're going right to it!" Spring squealed.

It was true. The rainbow was leading them straight to the blanket. They were going to pass right through it on the way to the ground!

"Grab it!" Summer screamed.

She and Winter both turned and dove headfirst with their arms stretched out in front of them. Autumn did the same. It was the first time she ever turned upside down in the rainbow, and it made her so dizzy she had to close her eyes a moment so she wouldn't get sick.

Here it came . . . closer . . . closer . . .

"Aggggghhhh!" Winter screamed.

They passed clean through the blanket as if it weren't even there.

Of course. Just like when they soared through Whisper's carriage canopy, just like *every* time they rode the rainbow, they couldn't touch anything around them. All the Sparkles knew this, but they were so eager to snatch Mother Nature's blanket that they forgot.

Autumn turned right side up again and squinted to keep her eyes on the blanket, but the rainbow's arc took them too far away. The blanket disappeared into the distance. Soon its tree was just one among hundreds, impossible to pick out.

Autumn was so concentrated on the blanket that she didn't even sense the rainbow's end. It ejected her with a *THUMP*, and she fell flat on her bottom into a foot of powdery snow. Falling snowflakes quickly coated her braid. Yet even though it was cold, Autumn wasn't uncomfortable. The temperatures in one another's realms never bothered the Sparkles. Winter never felt hot wearing her snowsuit in Summer's land, just like the other sisters felt perfectly warm wearing light clothes in the middle of a wintery blizzard.

"Nice dismount," Summer teased.

"We were *right there*," Autumn said. "Now we'll never find the blanket."

"Never say never in my realm!" Winter declared. "I know this Sparkledom, and I know *exactly* how to get back to that tree. Come on! Follow me!"

Winter strode across the landscape with giant steps. Her boots were natural snowshoes that carried her easily over the piles of powder. Summer and Autumn knew they couldn't follow, but stopping Winter when she had a full head of steam was nearly impossible. They were confident Winter would remember soon enough and come back for them.

Spring, however, had come out of the rainbow behind her sisters, and did not think as many steps ahead as Summer and Autumn. When Winter told them to follow, she obeyed, but her sandals were *not* natural snowshoes. She took one step and *crunched* into the snow. It buried her halfway to her knee. Not willing to give up, she took another long step . . . and *crunched* deeper into the snow. Still she kept going. She struggled to lift each leg out of its thick pile of snow, then swing it around and set it down once more.

She made it three steps before she tromped into Summer and Autumn's view. By then both her legs were buried as deep as her thighs and she couldn't move another inch. Summer and Autumn gasped when they saw her. "Spring, stop!" Autumn cried.

"I don't think I have a choice," Spring moaned.

"Winter!" Summer shouted. *"Winter! Spring needs you!"*

That stopped Winter in her tracks. She bounded back to her sisters. When she saw Spring, she smacked her forehead with her palm. "Snowshoes!" she remembered. "The three of you need snowshoes." She flung her head back as far as it could go and screamed, "Flurry! *FLURRY!* FLUUUUUUURRRR-RRRYYYYY!!!!"

Nothing.

Winter sighed, reached into her coat, and pulled out a candy cane. She peeled off the tiniest corner of its plastic wrapping.

Suddenly, the ground shook. A moment later, the world's largest polar bear bounded over the horizon, his tongue flapping behind him. He leaped into the air, threw himself onto his belly, and slid across the snow. He stopped right in front of Winter, nose to nose with his Sparkle. He widened his eyes to make himself extra cute and whined high in his throat.

"Really?" Winter said. "It had to be the candy? You couldn't just come when I called?"

Flurry batted his eyes and licked Winter's nose.

"It's yours," Winter said. "And there's one more if you bring my sisters' snowshoes from the chalet, okay?" Winter peeled off the rest of the wrapper, threw the candy cane as hard as she could, and cried, "Go get it, boy!"

Flurry raced after the treat. He grabbed it and gulped it down in midair, then disappeared into the distance. A long moment passed, so long that Winter's sisters weren't sure he was coming back. Then Winter grinned. "Three . . . two . . . one . . ."

Again the ground shook as Flurry zoomed toward them, only this time he pulled a sleigh behind him.

He tugged it by a long red strap he held in his mouth. He stopped in front of Winter, halted the sleigh with his paw, then showed off what was on the seat inside: three pairs of snowshoes. Job done, he sat up on his back legs and looked hopefully at his Sparkle.

"Snowshoes *and* a sleigh!" Winter enthused. "That's worth *two* candy canes." She unwrapped the treats and tossed them into his mouth. Flurry swallowed them in one delighted gulp, then happily fell back into the snow with a mighty *FOOMP*.

"You are ridiculous." Winter said it sternly, but she meant it with love. Flurry had been with her since he was so small he could fit in her palm. Aside from her sisters, he was her best friend in the world.

As Winter scratched Flurry's belly, Summer grabbed the three pairs of snowshoes off the sleigh. She and Autumn put theirs on first. Autumn felt very clumsy in the large snowshoes, but she managed them well enough to help Summer pull Spring out of her snow pile. As Spring put on her own shoes, Winter hooked Flurry to the sleigh, then her sisters climbed aboard. Winter herself jumped onto Flurry's back.

"Hey, Flurry," Winter said. "I just realized I left a huge stash of candy canes in a knothole of one of the trees. I'll tell you the way, and if you pull us there, half the stash is yours."

Flurry took off so quickly, Autumn had to clutch the sides of the sleigh so she wasn't thrown into the snow.

"Do you think this sleigh is safe?" she shouted over the whipping wind.

"No idea!" Summer shouted back. "But it sure is fun!"

"Fun" wasn't the word Autumn would have used, but it definitely was fast. Before she could truly register how completely terrified she was, Flurry had whipped the sleigh across miles of snowy landscape, up a staggeringly steep mountain, and pulled to a stop next to an evergreen.

"This is the one!" Winter cried, hopping off Flurry's back.

Autumn looked around. Winter was talking about

one tree at the edge of a giant copse of look-alikes, all with branches so high it was impossible to see them all. "How can you be sure?" she asked.

"I know my trees," Winter said. "Plus I'll show you." Winter beckoned her sisters over, then positioned them in just the right spot beneath the tree. "Look up . . . now tilt to the right . . . now crouch a little . . . now squint . . . now look through a bunch of branch layers to the one *all* the way . . ."

"I see it!" Spring squealed. "I see the blanket!"

Autumn did too, and she threw her arms around Winter. "Thank you," she said. "You are amazing."

"I *will* be amazing," she replied, "when I bring it down. Flurry, give me a boost! Flurry?"

When Winter had failed to pull candy canes from the tree's knothole, Flurry had gone nosing around, and found a large box of candy canes stashed under the sleigh seat. He promptly cuddled up in the snow to enjoy the prize. When Winter found him, his entire snout was pink, and half-eaten sticky canes clung to his face, paws, and neck. "Flurry?" she asked. "Are you going to help me?"

Flurry cuddled deeper into the snow, his tongue working around several candies at once.

"Flurry's out," Winter said, tromping back to the tree. "I'll get it myself."

She had only just started scrambling up the thick evergreen trunk when an ice-cold voice sliced into the Sparkles' ears.

"Get *what* yourself?"

The sisters wheeled around. An angry-looking boy stood with his hands on his hips, his glare pure ice.

It was Sleet, one of Bluster Tempest's Weeds and one of the Sparkles' greatest enemies. If he found out about Serenity's blanket, he'd do anything to steal it.

CHAPTER
5

Sleet slowly moved closer to the Sparkles.

He walked easily on the snow like Winter, but his shoes left dirty footprints. "You need to speak up. Whatever you're going to get, I might want to take. But first I need to know what it is."

Summer placed one hand on her scepter, ready to draw. "You're not taking anything from us, Sleet."

"That's right," Winter added, thumping down from the tree trunk, "because there's nothing to take. I was just teaching my sisters some climbing skills."

Sleet laughed. It sounded like ice clinking around in a glass. "I don't believe you," he said. "I think there's something in that tree. And if you want to keep it a secret, it's probably something very interesting." He tried to take another step forward, but Winter blocked his path.

"Why do you hang out in my realm so much, Sleet?" she asked. "You're not welcome here."

She stood toe-to-toe with the Weed. They were the exact same height, and they both flourished in wintery weather, but the similarities ended there. Unlike Winter, everything about Sleet looked cold and dangerous, from his blue-black spiked hair to his raincloud-gray clothes to his winter-storm eyes. His eyebrows pointed down in a wide V, so he always looked angry.

"I can go wherever I like," Sleet retorted. "And I can take whatever I find. Like the thing you're hiding. I bet I can get it before you."

"Good luck with that," Winter said.

"That's kind of you," Sleet replied, "but I won't need luck."

He feinted one way, then ran the other, dodging around Winter and leaping onto the tree trunk. Like all the Weeds, Sleet spent most of his time wrestling, climbing, running, and digging for trouble, so he was very fast—almost as quick as Summer and Winter. He scrambled up the tree so quickly it looked like he had extra arms and legs. Winter just watched him, which Autumn couldn't understand.

"Winter," she said nervously, "what if he gets the blanket?"

"He won't," Winter replied. Autumn wanted to believe her, but it was hard when Sleet was climbing higher and higher.

Finally, when he was about halfway up the trunk, Winter threw back her head and called, "WHOOOOO-OOP!"

Flurry was still licking candy cane from his fur, but when Winter hollered, he rose onto his hind legs, sauntered to the tree, reached up, and hooked a claw through the collar of Sleet's shirt. Sleet kicked his feet and shook his arms as the giant polar bear pulled him away from the tree and held him in midair. "Hey!" he cried. "Come on! You're supposed to play fair!"

"*Fair?*" Spring cried. "You're trying to steal Mother Nature's blanket!"

The instant she said it, her eyes went wide and she clapped her hands over her mouth.

Too late. Sleet stopped kicking and grinned.

"Mother Nature's blanket?" he said. "Interesting. That sounds like something you wouldn't want to lose. It also sounds like something Bluster would *looooove* to have."

"Tough talk from someone dangling in the air from a polar bear claw," Winter said.

"You think this bothers me?" Sleet asked. He pulled a short, twisted stick from his belt and pointed it into the air. Then he aimed it at Flurry's head and shouted, "*Scraggofrakakika!*"

A sleet storm poured down from the sky. It was aimed directly at Flurry. Keeping Sleet firmly in his claw, Flurry darted this way and that. He tried to get away from the ice, but it followed him wherever he went.

"Hurts, doesn't it?" Sleet laughed, untouched by the pummeling storm. "My ice is awfully sharp."

"I've got this," Summer said. She pulled out her scepter and chanted:

"To stop poor Flurry getting pelted,
Give me heat, get this sleet melted!"

A blaze of yellow sparkles shot from Summer's scepter and melted every bit of ice they touched, but it wasn't enough. The sleet kept coming, and Summer's sparkles couldn't keep up with it all. Flurry snapped at the icy barbs, batting them away with his free paw, but he was still getting pelted.

"Leave him alone!" Winter hollered.

"Of course!" Sleet said. "Give me the blanket!"

"Never!" Spring shouted.

Sleet shrugged as best as he could while hanging in midair from Flurry's claw. "So sad. Guess you don't really care about the bear."

He swirled his stick in the air, hollered another terrible spell, then snapped his wrist toward Flurry. Now the sleet fell harder and faster. Flurry whimpered. It was horrible to watch. Autumn couldn't take it. "Maybe we *should* give Sleet the blanket," she said.

"Forget it," Winter shot back. Then she called out, "Just get rid of him, Flurry! Now!"

Flurry gave a questioning growl, but when Winter nodded, the bear pulled back his paw and whipped it forward. Sleet screamed as he soared through the air, but the sound grew softer and softer as he disappeared into the faraway distance.

The sleet storm vanished.

Autumn, Spring, and Summer stared at Winter, openmouthed.

"Is Sleet okay?" Spring asked.

"Of course he's okay," Winter said. "We wouldn't actually *hurt* him." She scrambled up Flurry's back, stood on his head, and squinted into the distance. "There," she said. "He landed in a snowbank on the other side of the pond. He's fine. Now let me get the blanket before he comes back."

Winter leaped from Flurry's head to the highest branch she could reach. From there, she swung like an acrobat from limb to limb. More than once,

Winter came so close to falling that Autumn had to close her eyes. Finally, Winter jumped to the branch that held the blanket, and grabbed hold with both hands. It shook wildly with the weight of her swinging body.

"Is it going to break?" Spring asked worriedly.

"She won't be on it long," Summer said. "It'll hold her."

The branch bent even more as Winter swung herself up to a seated position. The blanket draped only a few feet away from her. All she needed to do was scoot a little bit closer . . .

Crack!

"Cobwebs and cockleshells!" Spring exclaimed. "Was that the branch?"

Neither Summer nor Autumn answered, but they each took one of Spring's hands as they all breathlessly watched Winter scoot the last inches between herself and the blanket.

CRACK!

The entire branch snapped clean off the tree. Both Winter and the blanket fell.

"NO!" Spring wailed.

The sisters were terrified, but Winter didn't seem frightened at all. Even as she plummeted, she reached for the blanket. Her fingers grazed it, but the wind whipped it away before she could get a firm grip.

"Blast!" she yelled, followed by "Ouch!" and "Oof!" as she smacked into several branches. None of them stopped her fall, and she was about to run out of branches and hurtle straight to the ground, when she grabbed the lowest tree branch with both hands. She dangled there, still so high she could look down at the top of Flurry's head.

"Winter!" Autumn called. "Are you okay?"

"No!" she called back.

"You're hurt?" Spring asked.

"Of course not—but I lost the blanket! Hey, Flurry—catch!"

She released the branch, and Flurry flopped onto his back so Winter could land with a giant *FOOMF* in the middle of his soft, furry belly. She crawled up his body until the two were face-to-face.

"Thanks, Flurry."

Flurry wrapped his paws around her and hugged her tight.

"Okay, okay." Winter laughed. "I need to breathe..."

"Are you sure you're okay?" Autumn asked.

"Perfectly," Winter assured her. "And I saw where the blanket went. Follow me!"

She took off running and Autumn stumbled over her snowshoes trying to keep up. Winter led her sisters to a clearing at the very edge of the mountaintop.

"We should be able to see it from here," Winter said. "Eyes peeled."

Winter was right. If the blanket was anywhere in the area, they'd see it from this spot. The view was dizzying. Far below them ran a fast-moving river surrounded by glaciers and thick sheets of ice. Autumn knew that eventually the river led to a tall waterfall that flowed into Spring's Sparkledom, but she couldn't see that from here.

Together, the sisters scanned horizon to horizon.

"There it is!" Summer cried.

Mother's present for Serenity danced in the wind,

halfway between the Sparkles above and the river below.

"I think it's going to land in the water," Autumn realized. "If I get down there, I can catch it!" She took one clumsy downhill snowshoe-step before Winter grabbed her arm.

"You can't just run down a mountain! Who do you think you are, me? Flurry, bring the sleigh!"

Flurry obeyed. Summer and Spring climbed aboard, but Autumn hesitated. Winter had done so much, but the blanket was Autumn's responsibility, and Autumn wanted to do her part to retrieve it. She had an idea, but it made her so nervous she knew she'd have to jump in and do it without thinking about it first.

"Winter, can I ride on Flurry with you? It'll give me a better view, and then you don't have to do anything but steer."

"You'll really ride up on Flurry?" Winter sounded surprised but thrilled. "That would be amazing! Ditch the snowshoes and hop aboard!"

Autumn did, but it wasn't easy. Even though

Flurry was about the same size as Whisper, the bear couldn't give Autumn the same elephant-trunk boost. She had to struggle to get astride him, and once she did, she felt strange and unbalanced. Flurry's back was so broad that Autumn couldn't grip with her legs. This, Autumn told herself, was why quick decisions were a bad idea. Riding on Flurry was a mistake. She should change her mind and get off. Now.

"AAAAAA!!!!!!"

Too late. Autumn screamed as Flurry raced down the impossibly steep slope. Autumn dug her fingers into Flurry's fur and gripped so hard her hands went numb. She tried to squeeze her legs around Flurry and steady herself, but she still bounced up so wildly she was positive she'd be thrown and tumble down to the river.

Autumn ached to shut her eyes and take deep breaths, but she wouldn't let herself. *She* lost Mother's blanket. She had to work to find it again. She steeled herself, sat up tall, and scanned the sky.

"THERE!" Autumn screamed. The blanket floated just above the rushing river, not far from them at all.

"Good eyes!" Winter cried. "Hold on tight!"

She swerved Flurry, and the sleigh whipped around behind him. Autumn screamed, but she kept her eyes locked on the blanket as Flurry zoomed onto a wide, flat sheet of ice that ended at the very edge of the river.

Flurry ran easily on snow, but ice was much harder. He slipped and slid and made little progress. The blanket, meanwhile, came to rest at the very edge of the ice sheet. It dangled there, one corner in the rushing river. If Autumn didn't act quickly, it would rush away with the current and she'd never see it again. Without thinking, she leaped off Flurry's back and raced across the ice, but her feet slid fruitlessly.

She had no time for this. With a wild burst of inspiration, she threw herself on her stomach and slid across the ice. She sailed to a stop just inches away from the blanket. It twinkled in front of her, teasing her with its closeness. One last lunge and she'd have it back. She hurled her body forward . . .

. . . just as a gust of wind blew the blanket into the

river. Autumn could only gape as the rushing water whisked it around a bend and out of sight.

"That was *amazing*!" Winter cried.

Autumn turned and saw her three sisters approaching. Winter looked so happy she practically glowed.

"What are you talking about?" Autumn asked. "I didn't get the blanket."

"But you rode Flurry! And you jumped off him! And you slid on the ice like a seal! That's so . . . not you!" Winter seemed to realize that didn't sound quite right, so she added, "No offense."

"It's okay," Autumn said. "You're right. I didn't really think about what I was doing. I just wanted to get the blanket."

"We still can," Summer said. "I have an idea." She raised her scepter and cried:

> "The summer sun can cut and slice,
> To make a raft that's cold as ice!"

She touched her scepter to the ice behind them.

Yellow sparkles spread over it in a long line until the sheet of ice cracked away and became a raft that hurled into the river with a tumbling jolt. Back on the shore Flurry roared, but his voice grew softer as the float raced the Sparkles down the churning river.

"It's okay, sweet little bear!" Spring called to him. "We know what we're doing!" Then she turned to Summer. "Um . . . what exactly are we doing?"

"White-water rafting!" Winter crowed. "Summer, you're brilliant!"

"I can't let you and Autumn be the only ones trying crazy things to get the blanket, can I?" Summer winked at Autumn, and Autumn felt strangely proud to be included as a fellow adventurer.

They all screamed as the ice raft hurtled around a corner, but then they saw the blanket again. It was far ahead of them, and moving quickly.

"How can we possibly catch up to it?" Autumn asked.

No one had an answer.

"Winter," Spring asked, "do you think I can take off my snowshoes? They're kind of uncomfortable."

Autumn knew what she meant. She was glad she'd already removed her own snowshoes. They were so big and unwieldy. Like giant oars on her feet.

Giant oars.

"Winter!" Autumn cried. "Can you freeze the snowshoes solid?"

"You really think that'll make them more comf—" Winter's eyes lit up as she got it. "Solid like paddles! Yes! Summer, Spring, take off the snowshoes!"

They did, and Winter pulled out her scepter.

"For these shoes to truly please,
I need to make them truly freeze!"

Blue sparkles shot out and danced over all four snowshoes, turning exactly half of each into solid ice.

"Just half?" Autumn asked.

"The other half's the handle," Winter said. "Now everyone grab a paddle and row!"

Each sister grabbed a snowshoe-paddle and rowed through the choppy river. Freezing water

splashed in their faces. Churning rapids threatened to throw them overboard. Still, they kept going, getting closer and closer to the blanket. When they were just behind it, Winter reached out with her paddle, stretching it as far as she could.

"I'm so close!" she said. "I can almost get it!"

Spring tapped Autumn's back and said something Autumn couldn't hear over the roar of the water.

"Paddle harder, everyone!" Summer called. "Get Winter closer!"

Autumn paddled harder. She thought she might

have heard Spring say something else, but she wasn't sure.

"I've got it!" Winter cried as her paddle caught the blanket's edge, but before she could pull it in, a dip in the river jolted the blanket away.

"No!" Winter, Summer, and Autumn all moaned.

"AUTUMN, SUMMER, AND WINTER!!!!" Spring shrieked. "Please listen to me!"

Spring never yelled like that. All three sisters turned to her. Now that she had their attention, she spoke softly. She said only one word.

"Waterfall."

They'd been so focused on the blanket they hadn't even realized, but now they turned and saw it. Just a short way down the river, everything disappeared over the giant waterfall that connected Winter's Sparkledom to Spring's.

The sisters barely had time to scream. First the blanket slipped over the waterfall's edge, then the ice raft and the Sparkles plunged down after it.

CHAPTER
6

Autumn's eyes were closed. She was falling. Her back hit something soft and springy, then she was in the air again.

It didn't make sense. Shouldn't she have plummeted into the water in Spring's realm?

Her back hit the soft, springy thing again.

Now Autumn heard something. Screams. Oh, no. Were her sisters okay? But there was something else too. Could it be . . . laughter?

"Autumn, open your eyes!" Winter said. "Spring caught us!"

Autumn looked around. She was sitting on a giant net made of vines and covered with fluffy moss and flowers. The net stretched from a tall tree on one riverbank to an even taller tree on the other.

"You grew this?" Autumn asked Spring. "But you were so scared..." Like all the Sparkles, Spring usually had trouble with her powers when she was very emotional.

"Oh, I wasn't scared," Spring said. "I mean, I was at first, but then I thought about the word 'waterfall,' and how perfect it is that it's exactly what it describes: *water...falling!* And then I thought about other words that do the same thing, like 'afternoon,' which comes *after noon*, and 'cupcake,' which is a *cake* in a *cup*, and—"

Winter laughed. "Spring, we'd have gone over the falls by the time you thought all that."

"But it's true!" Spring insisted. "And then I thought the word 'waterfall' would be perfect for a way into your Sparkledom, Autumn, because then it would be *water, fall*ing into *fall*! And then I remembered—we were falling into *spring*! My home! And I couldn't be scared falling into my own Sparkledom. So while we were falling, I used my powers to make us a soft landing spot. Do you like it?"

"I *love* it," Autumn said. "Did you catch the blanket too?"

"Sorry," Spring said. "It fell too quickly. But it has to be down there somewhere, right?"

Autumn looked down. As always, Spring's land was sunny and beautiful. Countless flowers bloomed, and the fields were filled with adorable baby animals. The lagoon into which the waterfall spilled was filled with life too. Baby ducks glided along the surface, while underwater, schools of fish swam every which way. The lagoon was so clear that Autumn could see all the way to the bottom.

The blanket wasn't there.

"I don't see it," Autumn said. "It must have floated down one of those paths."

She pointed to the far end of the lagoon, where the water split into four streams. Each branched off to a different part of Spring's Sparkledom.

"So we'll check them all," Winter said.

"We don't have time," Summer said. "Look at the sky. It's already late in the afternoon, and Serenity's party's at sunset."

"We'll split up," Autumn said. "We'll each explore a different branch of the river. When one of us finds the blanket, we'll send the rainbow for the others. We just have to get down from this net first."

"I know how," Spring said. She whistled. The Sparkles heard hoofbeats and a loud neigh, then a beautiful violet unicorn appeared on the bank of the lagoon.

"Dewdrop!" Spring squealed.

Spring loved every animal, but Dewdrop was by far her favorite. He was the only creature of his kind. Mother Nature had given him to Spring when Dewdrop was a baby with a teeny bump for a horn. Flowers grew naturally in Dewdrop's mane and tail, and though he was fully grown, he still acted like a baby. His favorite thing was lying with his head in Spring's lap while she scratched him to sleep.

"Can you give us a ride, Dewdrop?" Spring asked.

Dewdrop neighed what could only be a yes, then took a running start and leaped. Dewdrop didn't have wings, but he could leap so high and long it was just like flying. When he was just below the net, all four Sparkles leaped onto his back. Dewdrop carried them effortlessly, then landed on the lagoon bank near the start of the four streams.

It was time to split up. Even though it had been her idea, Autumn was worried. She hadn't forgotten about Sleet. What if he had already told the other Weeds—or worse—Bluster Tempest about the blanket? What if they were looking for the blanket too?

"Maybe I was wrong," Autumn said. "Maybe we shouldn't go off on our own."

"You're right!" Spring said brightly. She tilted her head back and made a series of impossibly high-pitched squeals. Seconds later, four pink dolphins popped their heads out of the lagoon and echoed the sounds exactly.

"Thanks for coming!" Spring said. "Can you give us rides down the streams? It's to help Mother Nature."

The dolphins all chirped and did backflips.

"They said they'd love to," Spring translated. "Hop on!"

Each Sparkle climbed aboard a dolphin. Once they were settled, Autumn said, "The minute one of us sees the blanket, we call the others by rainbow, right?"

"Right," Summer agreed. Then she leaned down

to her dolphin and asked, "So . . . how fast can you go?"

The dolphin squealed, then tore down one branch of the river.

"You think that's fast?" Winter cried. "Show 'em what you can do, dolphin!"

Winter's dolphin screeched excitedly, then raced down a second stream.

"Slow down!" Autumn called after them. "You can't look for the blanket if you're going that fast!"

"Don't worry," said Spring. "They won't miss it."

"But they're not even paying attention," Autumn said. "They're just racing!"

"They'll pay attention when it's important," Spring said.

"How do you know?" Autumn asked.

Spring shrugged. "I trust them."

She chirped to her dolphin, and the two traveled a slow, S-shaped pattern down a third stream. Dewdrop trotted on the shore beside them.

"I see it!" Spring gasped.

"Already?" Autumn asked. "You see the blanket?"

"No! A starfish with seven arms! And look, this anemone had babies! And they're purple!"

Autumn sighed. While Summer and Winter might zip right over the blanket, Spring could spend all day entranced by a single spot. If Autumn was lucky, the blanket would be in her own branch of the stream. She nickered to her dolphin, and they started their journey.

As they traveled, Spring's words echoed in Autumn's head. She'd said she trusted their sisters to pay attention when it was important. Truthfully, Autumn did too. With all four of them working together, they were sure to find Mother Nature's blanket.

They just had to find it in time.

CHAPTER
7

Autumn had been right to trust her sisters. Every one of them searched carefully for the blanket. And while each Sparkle wanted to be the one to find it, Spring wanted it most of all. She wanted her sisters to be proud of her. She hadn't seen a trace of the blanket yet, and it was getting late, but Spring wasn't worried. She was in her own Sparkledom. Things worked for her here.

"We'll find it, right, Dewdrop?" she asked. The unicorn clip-clopped down the riverbank through a patch of fluffy dandelions. Mother once told Spring that in the Outworlders' realm, dandelion fluff was always white. How sad that must be! Dandelion tops in Spring's realm not only grew as large and round as Spring's own head, but they came in every color:

yellow, blue, pink . . . even orange-and-purple polka dots.

Dewdrop sneezed as the fluff tickled his nose, and multicolored dandelion fluff flew everywhere. Spring giggled as the feathery seed pods whirled around her, then she suddenly gasped.

"Fluff and feathers, Dewdrop!" she cried. "You gave me an idea! We can *wish* for the blanket!"

While dandelions in the Sparkledoms and the Outworld couldn't be more different, they did have one thing in common: both were perfect for wishes. Spring urged her dolphin to the riverbank until they were face-to-fluff with the lowest-hanging flowers. "When I say 'wish' the second time we all blow," she told Dewdrop and the dolphin. "That'll make it a triple-wish." She closed her eyes tight and said, "We wish to find Mother Nature's blanket. Dish . . . fish . . . *wish*!"

Spring, Dewdrop, and the dolphin all blew. When Spring opened her eyes, she saw the whole world through twinkly specks of dancing rainbow fluff. Everything looked so magical, Spring was sure their

wish would come true. She urged her dolphin onward, already imagining herself holding that beautiful blanket in her hands.

Dewdrop saw it first. The minute they rounded a bend, he neighed and stomped his feet. He was so excited that Spring would've known exactly what he meant even if she couldn't speak Unicorn.

"You did it, Dewy!" Spring squealed.

The blanket was caught in a knot of branches at the river's edge. Spring carefully untangled it while perched on her dolphin. She had to work slowly so the blanket wouldn't tear, and Dewdrop had to use his horn to loosen the trickiest snarls, but soon it was free, and as gorgeous as Spring remembered it. She hugged it close, enjoying its silky feel against her cheek.

"Wait until I tell my sisters!" Spring enthused. She grabbed Dewdrop's horn for balance and climbed onto the riverbank, then reached her scepter high into the air.

"Careful where you point that thing," a boy's voice warned. "You could hurt someone."

Spring screamed and spun around, hiding the blanket behind her back. She looked for the source of the voice, but all she saw was a bush with swirl-shaped flowers. The flower on top was orange.

"That's funny," she told Dewdrop. "I don't remember an orange flower on that bush."

Then the orange flower moved. It rose up until Spring saw it wasn't a flower at all, but the swirl of hair on top of Twister, one of the Weeds. "My apologies," Twister said as he stepped away from the bush. "I didn't mean to scare you."

Twister wore high brown boots, short pants, a

yellow shirt, and a long, high-collared coat. His hair scorpion-curled to a tall point above his head. His bushy orange eyebrows moved a lot when he talked. He moved closer to Spring and bowed low. "I do hope you can excuse my intrusion into your Sparkle-dom."

Spring was charmed by Twister's manners and almost invited him to her home for a tea party, but then she reminded herself that he was a Weed. He had to be up to no good. He might have even been sent by Sleet to look for Mother's blanket. Keeping her hands behind her back, Spring tucked the precious item in the folds of her dress.

"Consider yourself excused," Spring said. "And now it's your turn to excuse me. Dewdrop and I have to go."

Yet before she could hop onto Dewdrop and fly somewhere far enough away to call her sisters, Twister sighed.

It was a terrible sigh, filled with sorrow, and it pierced Spring's heart. Only something horribly sad could inspire a sigh like that.

"Are you okay?" Spring asked.

"What?" Twister jumped, surprised. "Oh, I'm sorry. I didn't mean for you to hear that. I was just hoping I could show you something, but if you have to go . . ." He sighed again, and Spring could feel his heartache as if it were her own.

"I guess I could stay for a minute," Spring said.

"Really?" Twister said. His eyes glowed with hope, and Spring felt proud to be the cause.

"Of course! What would you like to show me?"

"How I play with hummingbirds," he said. He beckoned her toward the bush, where several hummingbirds flitted around the flowers. Then Twister pulled out his gnarled stick of a wand.

"Oh, no!" Spring gasped. She backed away, but Twister touched her arm gently.

"It's okay," Twister assured her. "I promise." He pointed the stick at the bush and whispered, "*Swivveleeood.*" Suddenly, several hummingbird-size tornadoes appeared in the air. Spring almost cried out again, but then she realized the hummingbirds weren't frightened. They were fascinated. They flew close to the tiny windstorms, then moved with the storms in playful unison.

"They're dancing with the baby storms!" Spring cried. "It's so adorable!"

"Isn't it?" Twister agreed.

The two of them stood in companionable silence a moment, happily watching the birds. Then Twister cleared his throat. He shuffled his feet and looked at the ground as he asked, "Um . . . Spring? Can I ask you a question?"

"Is the question 'If flies can fly, and ducks can duck, and bees can be . . . why can't otters otter?'"

"Um . . . no."

"Oh, good," Spring said, "because I don't know the answer to that one."

"I was wondering," Twister began, "if you would join me for a picnic."

"A picnic?"

"That's the other reason I came here," Twister said. "I like picnics, and there are no good picnic spots in the Barrens. I thought I'd picnic by myself, but a picnic's a lot more fun when you share it with someone."

Spring agreed. She certainly didn't want Twister to have a picnic all alone, but how could she join him? Her sisters were still looking for the blanket. They had no idea Spring had found it. She needed to call them and let them know.

"It's okay." Twister sighed. "It was a silly question. You probably wouldn't want to have a picnic with a Weed anyway."

He dropped his head lower. He looked so sad Spring thought it would rip her apart. She looked up at the sun. It was late, but she did have the blanket, so she and her sisters weren't really in a hurry. Spring knew it wasn't right to keep the other Sparkles waiting, but she just couldn't leave Twister all alone when he looked so miserable.

"I'd love to have a picnic with you," she said, "but I can only stay for a minute."

"Truly?" A huge smile lit up Twister's face. "That's great!"

He reached behind the bush and pulled out a large basket made of sticks and rocks. "I made it myself," he said proudly. "And it's filled with delicious food!"

He lifted one side of the basket top. It didn't smell delicious to Spring. It smelled more like feet.

"I'm not really hungry," she said, "but I'm happy to sit with you."

"Wonderful," Twister said.

But he didn't sit. He just looked at the ground.

"Is everything okay?" Spring asked.

"Oh, yes! I just wish . . ." Twister sighed. "I wish we had a picnic blanket. It's not really a picnic without a picnic blanket."

"That's true," Spring agreed. "Oh! I know! I'll ride Dewdrop and get a blanket from my castle!"

"That's okay." Twister stopped her. "I'd rather have the company. It only made sense if you had a blanket nearby. You know, for a proper picnic." He sighed again, then added, "Ah well. You get what you get and you don't get upset."

He plopped down on the ground and started setting up the meal. For Spring, that settled it. Twister might be a Weed, but he was *not* like the others. He was nice! He deserved a proper picnic, even if it was just for a couple minutes.

"I just remembered!" Spring chirped. "I *do* have a blanket!" She took Mother's blanket from the folds of her dress. "It's not really mine, so we can't sit on it, but we can lay it down." She shook out the blanket and spread it gently on the grass. "How's that?"

"Perfect," Twister said. He smiled, and the corners of his mouth curled in a mean funnel shape Spring hadn't noticed before. A tiny prickle of alarm played on the back of her neck, but it was too late.

"*Swooriviroonu!*" Twister cried.

With a flick of his wand, a thick black tornado swirled up from the ground, scooped up Twister and Mother's blanket, and whooshed them both out of sight.

CHAPTER
8

What were you *thinking*?" Winter roared.

Once Twister left, Spring had called her sisters by rainbow so she could explain what had happened. They were all stunned, but Winter was having the most trouble understanding it. Spring answered her question as best she could.

"Well," Spring said, "first I was thinking he is a Weed and I shouldn't trust him, but then I was thinking he seemed so nice and so sad about not having a proper picnic. And then at one point I was thinking about how funny it is that both halves of the word 'picnic' rhyme: *pic-nic*. And I was thinking of other words like that, like 'backpack' or 'tepee'..."

"*SPRING!*" Winter exploded.

"But mostly I was thinking about the way you'd

sound when you heard how badly I messed up,"
Spring added sadly.

"You didn't mess up, Spring," Autumn assured
her. "I did. I lost Mother's blanket. You were just trying to help. All three of you were. Thank you."

She gave each of her sisters a big hug, then raised
her scepter in the air. She knew what she had to do.

"Oh, no," Winter said, catching her arm. "I know
what you're thinking, but no way. You're not going to
tell Mother. Not yet."

"I have to," Autumn said. "The blanket was my
responsibility. It was up to me to keep it safe, and I
didn't. I have to tell Mother the truth."

Too painful to say out loud were the words
Autumn added inside her head: *Even if it means
Mother never trusts me again.*

"Winter's right. This isn't over yet. We can still
find the blanket," Summer said. She had wandered
off a short distance, and stared at a patch of bushes.
"The damage from Twister's tornado makes a path,
and it doesn't lead to the Barrens. It leads toward my
Sparkledom."

"Why would Twister take the blanket to your Sparkledom?" Winter asked.

"Maybe he wanted a *beach* picnic!" Spring bubbled.

"Doubt that," Summer said. "But maybe he was running so fast he got turned around inside his tornado. Whatever the reason, if he's in my Sparkledom, I can find him. I know that place better than any Weed."

"I don't know," Autumn said. "The three of you have already gone through so much for me . . ."

"We're your sisters," Summer said. "That's what we do. So what do you say? Will you let me try this before you go to Mother?"

"I will," Autumn agreed. "Thank you."

"Perfect! Spring, can I borrow Dewdrop? I can surprise Twister better if I'm alone."

"Dewy would be honored," Spring said.

"Great. Once I leave, the three of you can follow the tornado damage trail and meet up with me. See it?"

Summer showed her sisters a jagged line of

windbeaten bushes and trees. The damage zig-zagged in a path all the way to the horizon line, where Spring's and Summer's Sparkledoms met.

"On it," Winter said. "We'll be right behind you."

Spring kissed Dewdrop's snout. "Have a fun trip, Dewy, and take good care of Summer."

Summer climbed onto the unicorn's back. Dewdrop took a running start, then leaped into the air. From this vantage point, Twister's damage trail was even easier to see. Summer guided the flying unicorn along until they reached the jungle that separated Spring's Sparkledom and her own. There Dewdrop landed and neighed. Summer could tell he wanted to stay in his own realm.

"Okay, Dewdrop," Summer said as she jumped off his back. "You did great. Thanks."

She broke off a wild sugarcane stalk and held it in her palm. Dewdrop took it gently into his mouth, nuzzled Summer's cheek, then flew off to rejoin Spring and the other Sparkles.

The jungle between Summer's and Spring's Sparkledoms was very long, stretching all across their border, but it wasn't thick. Summer followed Twister's trail through it, and soon emerged at the top of a large bluff. She took a deep breath of her home's salty air and looked down at the familiar wide fields of brown-tipped grass, the shimmering lakes, the white-, pink-, and black-sand beaches, and the endless roll of ocean waves.

The scenery was great, but right now Summer had a job to do, and it just got a lot harder. Now that she was out of the jungle, she had no trail to follow. Luckily, Summer knew where to find a pair of eyes a lot stronger than hers. She stuck two fingers in her mouth and blew a loud whistle: *WHOOP! WHOOP-per-WHOOP!*

Within seconds, and without making a sound, Summer's jaguar, Shade, appeared by her side. Shade was built like a hunter, sleek and low to the ground. Her spots were shaped like tiny suns.

"Hey, fierce girl," Summer whispered. The nickname was Summer's little joke. Shade could be tough and she had razor-sharp teeth, but she was sweet as a kitten. The scariest thing about her was her jackhammer-loud purr. She purred now as she rubbed her head against Summer and Summer scratched behind her ears. "Twister's somewhere in the Sparkledom," Summer said. "I need to know where."

Shade's ears perked up. Her tail and whiskers twitched as she scanned the horizon, left to right. Suddenly she stiffened. The fur on her back stood straight up, and her purr became a low growl. She leaned forward, her entire body now an arrow for Summer to follow.

"Yes," Summer said. "I see him."

Twister was far below, running quickly through a sparsely wooded area. He had a huge head start on Summer, but the Sparkle had a major advantage. She jumped onto Shade's back. The jaguar knew exactly what to do. Soundlessly, she raced down the hill and among the trees. From down here Summer couldn't see Twister at all, but she trusted Shade's senses.

Finally, she saw him far up ahead, darting from tree to tree as if too exhausted to keep moving. Each time he stopped, he looked around to make sure he was alone. Summer smiled. She felt confident she could catch him on her own from here. She slipped off Shade's back and whispered, "My sisters are on their way. Meet them at the border and bring them to me."

Shade ran off to obey, while Summer continued the chase. She pushed herself to close the distance between herself and the Weed. Every time Twister stumbled, Summer grinned. Every root seemed to break his stride, but Summer felt this land in her bones. Nothing slowed her down. Soon Summer was so close she could almost reach out and touch Twister's coat.

It was time. Summer reached for her scepter.

CRACK!

A giant tree branch snapped, fell, and landed right in front of Summer. It happened so quickly she couldn't stop moving. She tripped over it and fell face-first into the dirt.

Cackling laughter rang out from above her. It sounded like the squeal of someone sucking on a helium balloon. Summer knew the sound.

"Thunderbolt!" she roared.

"You called?" the Weed laughed. He floated on a low storm cloud that drifted out from its hiding spot, behind the high canopy of the same tree whose branch he'd broken off. The cloud was as dark as Thunderbolt's ratty black pants and jacket. His hair was purple and spiked, he wore a black shirt slashed with a purple lightning bolt, and his normally pale face was red from wheezy laughter. Summer tried to leap to her feet when she saw him, but she'd twisted her ankle in the fall. She winced and dropped to her knees, which only made Thunderbolt laugh harder.

Summer raised her scepter and pointed it at his cloud.

"Laugh it up, you nasty Weed,
Till you lose the thing you need."

A burst of yellow sparkles shot from her scepter into Thunderbolt's cloud. It disappeared instantly. Thunderbolt thumped to the ground.

"Hey!" he yelled. "What did you do that for? I never did nothing to you!"

"Except blast a branch with a lightning bolt so I'd trip on it?" Summer asked.

"Yeah!" he said. "Except that!"

"Don't argue with her, Thunderbolt." The voice was Twister's. He stepped out from behind a nearby tree. He had a nasty smile on his face. "We have her exactly where we want her."

Summer understood now, and the pain in her ankle was nothing compared to the torture of knowing she'd been outsmarted by Weeds—in her own Sparkledom! She wasn't giving up though, and there was no way she'd let Twister and Thunderbolt see how upset she really was.

"Yeah, you're both really impressive," Summer said. "Now give me the blanket and get out of here before I vaporize something else."

"*This* blanket?" Twister asked. He pulled it from his coat pocket and wiped his sweaty face, then held it out to Summer. "Here you go."

Ew. The blanket had Weed sweat on it now, but it was still Mother's. Summer reached for it, but as she was about to pinch the corner between her fingers, Twister nodded to someone behind her.

"Now, Quake," he said.

Summer spun just in time to see Quake holler and wave his stick in the air.

She heard the noise first. It was a deep rumble that shook her bones. Then the ground split beneath her. She tumbled backward, bouncing and rolling until she thumped down on the bottom of the newly created hole.

When the shaking stopped, Summer looked up. All four Weeds peered down at her. Even Sleet, who must have been waiting for the right moment to show his face. They looked so proud of themselves. Summer wondered if Shade had found the other Sparkles, and if they were on their way. Summer hoped so. She also hoped she could keep the Weeds right here and distracted until her sisters arrived.

"I'm starting to see why the four of you have no friends," Summer shouted up to them. "Hanging out with you is really annoying."

"We won't be in your hair much longer," Twister called down. "In fact, we'd like to offer you a deal. We know you want this blanket, and we will gladly give it to you. All you have to do in return is toss us your scepter."

Summer laughed out loud.

"Seriously? That's your big plan? Keep the blanket. No way am I giving you my scepter."

"You will, because if you don't . . ." Twister gave a sad sigh Spring would have recognized. "Sleet told me you saw what he did to the polar bear. That was nothing compared to what he'll rain down on you. And Thunderbolt has his own special skill to share."

"*Zizzlzzlzz!*" Thunderbolt yelled. He shot a bolt of lightning from his stick into the hole. It exploded into the ground only a hop away from Summer. The bolt hadn't touched her, but she could feel its heat and smell the electric sizzle.

"I'll give you to the count of five," Twister said. "One . . . two . . . three . . . "

Summer took a deep breath. She wiped her sweaty palm on her dress so she could clench her scepter tightly. She could *not* lose the scepter to the Weeds. She'd fight back as long as she could, and hope her sisters would show up before it was too late.

CHAPTER
9

Summer didn't know it, but her sisters were already there. Shade had met them at the border between Summer's and Spring's Sparkledoms, then had the girls climb on her back so she could get them to Summer as fast as possible. They were still on their way when they heard the *CRACK* of the tree limb breaking, the thump of Summer's fall, and electric Weed laughter.

"Summer!" Spring gasped.

"We have to help her!" Winter insisted. "Shade, run!"

Panic coursed through Autumn, but she forced herself to remain calm and firm. "*Don't* run, Shade," she said. "And Winter, Spring, please keep your voices down."

"What are you talking about?" Winter whisper-growled. "Summer needs us!"

"I agree. But didn't you hear that laugh?" Autumn asked. "That wasn't Twister. That was Thunderbolt. Something strange is going on here, and we shouldn't do anything until we know exactly what it is."

"No," Winter said. "This isn't time for one of your Autumn planning sessions. We have to *do* something."

"Winter, please, listen to me," Autumn pleaded. "I did things today I've never done. I rode a bear, I slid across a sheet of ice, I rafted down a river . . . I know you're right—sometimes you need to jump in and do something. But this isn't one of those times. I'm sure of it. I tried things your way. Can you please try them mine?"

Winter struggled with herself, but relented. "Fine. We plan. Any ideas?"

"We go somewhere we can see everything," said Autumn. "Someplace hidden, but close enough that we can jump in and help Summer when we need to. Shade?"

Shade thought, then darted through the woods and climbed up a sprawling tree thick with leaves that would give the Sparkles cover. The jaguar crawled to the edge of a lower limb. The Sparkles peered through the leaves and saw Summer on the ground not far away. Her face and dress were spattered with dirt. She glared up at Thunderbolt and Twister, who stood in front of her.

"Now, Quake," Twister said.

The Sparkles clutched one another as the short, pig-nosed Weed stepped forward and shouted his awful spell. Autumn squeezed her sisters' arms tightly as his earthquake split the ground and swallowed Summer whole. She knew Winter and Spring wanted to scream as much as she did, but silence had never been so important.

After the quake, the world felt terrifyingly still and silent. Was Summer okay?

Before they found out, Sleet emerged from the woods and joined his fellow Weeds. Winter shook her head in disbelief. "All four of them," she whispered to Autumn. "You were right. If we'd run out when I said, we'd be stuck in that hole with Summer."

Autumn couldn't respond. She was holding her breath, and only let it out when she heard Summer taunt the Weeds from inside the hole.

Summer was okay. That was good. But she still needed their help, and only a perfect plan would do. Autumn was so lost in her own thoughts she didn't hear what was happening below. She was surprised when Spring gasped and clapped a hand to her own mouth to stop from crying out.

"What happened?" Autumn asked.

"Twister told Summer that Sleet and Thunderbolt are going to blast her with their powers until she turns over her scepter," Winter replied, her mouth a thin angry line.

"That was the plan all along," Autumn realized. "Twister only took the blanket from Spring to lure us into a trap."

"I'll give you to the count of five," Twister warned Summer below. "One . . ."

Autumn had to think fast. Information, she needed information.

She studied the Weeds. As Twister spoke, Sleet stepped to the edge of the hole and cracked his knuckles. They popped like ice, and Autumn noticed Quake wince at the sound and give Sleet a dirty look.

"Two . . . ," Twister continued.

Thunderbolt hummed excitedly. Autumn saw Twister glare at him to stop, but that only made Thunderbolt hum even louder.

"Three . . . ," Twister said through gritted teeth.

Sleet was still cracking his knuckles, but Autumn realized he was now doing it closer to Quake's head. Quake balled his hands into fists and shuddered at every pop.

The Weeds might be working together, but they weren't a real team like the Sparkles. In fact, they seemed to love making one another crazy.

The gears were churning now in Autumn's mind, and a moment later she grabbed her sisters' arms. "I have it!" she declared. "The perfect plan."

Winter, Spring, and even Shade leaned in close, and Autumn quickly told them exactly what to do. She'd only just finished when Twister hollered, "*FIVE!*"

"*Fleggrambaaaa!*" Sleet roared. Yet just as he aimed his stick toward Summer, Autumn chanted a quick spell of her own and flicked her scepter toward Quake. A strong gust of wind hit him in the back. It blew him into Sleet, who lost his aim and shot his spell not at Summer, but at Twister.

Icy sleet pelted Twister. He screamed as he twisted and squirmed to fight off the storm. "*HEY!* What are you doing?"

"It was him!" Sleet said, pointing at Quake. "He pushed me!"

"Did not!" Quake cried. "It was an accident!"

"Oh, yeah?" Sleet said. "So's *this*! *Phregnoble-gacker!*"

He flicked his stick at Quake, and a fierce jet of sleet pummeled Quake's belly. Quake yelled a spell of his own, and the ground under Sleet became an endless personal earthquake. The shaking ground moved with Sleet and rattled his body so violently that the Sparkles could hear his chattering teeth from up in their tree.

Twister, meanwhile, still struggled under Sleet's storm. He screamed at his brother to make it stop, but Sleet was in no shape to stop anything, including his own wildly shaking body.

Only Thunderbolt was untouched. He laughed so hard at his brothers' misfortune he couldn't even stand. He fell over and rolled on the ground, gasping for air.

"Thunderbolt!" Twister roared. "Get up and get the Sparkle!"

"I will!" Thunderbolt panted through his laughter. "Look, I'll even get a running start."

He raced toward Summer's hole crying a wild spell, but his shout became a scream thanks to Spring. A little Sparkle Power from her, and a small root in Thunderbolt's path wrapped itself around the Weed's ankle. He flew forward, and his thunderbolt zapped off course to hit Twister right in the rear end.

"OW!" Twister wailed. "*Shaggrofligag!*"

He flicked his stick, and a tornado whirled out of the ground and scooped Thunderbolt off his feet. The Weed screamed as he spun around and around.

While the Weeds sank into chaos, Shade climbed down from the tree, Winter pressed low on her back. At the edge of Summer's hole, Winter lowered a vine Spring had grown for just this purpose, and Summer used it to pull herself out. The two girls quickly slipped back onto Shade, and the jaguar nimbly returned them to the safety of the tree branch. Once Summer slid off Shade, she wrapped her arms around all three of her sisters. "I knew you'd come save me," she said. "The Weeds are no match for the three of you."

"The *one* of us," Spring said. "It was all Autumn's plan."

"But it took all of us to carry it out," Autumn clarified.

"Still, it wouldn't have happened without you," Winter said. "So if I ever give you a hard time for planning again, you have my permission to smack me with a fish."

It was Winter's way of saying she was sorry.

Autumn didn't need an apology, but it made her feel warm inside all the same.

"So what's your next plan?" Summer asked Autumn. "How do we get the blanket from Twister?"

"We don't." Autumn's voice was gentle but firm. "It's not worth it. Let's just go to Mother's."

"But if you don't have the blanket, Mother will be so disappointed," Spring said.

"I know," Autumn agreed.

"But won't that make you feel terrible?" Spring asked.

"*Very* terrible," Autumn acknowledged, "but that's okay. I made a mistake, and sometimes when you make a mistake, you have to feel terrible for a little while. But I won't feel terrible forever. And next time I won't make the same mistake. Now let's go. There might not be a blanket, but there's still a party, and we don't want to miss it."

Together, the four Sparkles raised their scepters and began the chant that would take them to Mother's realm. They said it softly so the Weeds wouldn't hear.

Unfortunately, the Sparkles didn't realize what the

Weeds were up to. Once Summer returned to the group, the girls had stopped paying attention to the boys, and had no idea how drastically the situation below had changed.

It started with Twister, who was so furious at how badly his brothers had mucked things up that he ignored the sleet that still pelted him. He stared balefully at his brothers, all writhing and howling under one another's spells.

"Enough!" he snapped. "This ends now. We stop all the magic together. *Immediately.*"

He raised his own stick. The other Weeds heeded the fury in Twister's voice and did the same. They shouted their spells in unison, and the sleet, tornado, and earthquake disappeared, leaving the boys to dust themselves off and nurse their wounds and motion sickness.

"No more shenanigans," Twister continued. "We call Bluster. By the time he arrives, we'll have Summer's scepter, and the greatest victory he's ever known."

Twister raised his stick once more, and again the

other Weeds followed suit. They touched their sticks together and hollered in a single voice, "Bluster!"

With their boss on his way, Twister stalked to the edge of the hole. He was done playing games with Summer. He planned to attack her with the largest tornado he could summon. That would knock her out, and Twister would easily take her scepter. He aimed his gnarled wand into the hole . . . and gaped.

"Where is she?" he roared. "Where's the Sparkle? We've already called Bluster!"

The Weeds searched frantically until Quake spotted them: all four Sparkles and a jaguar, standing together on the same tree branch. The four Sparkles held their scepters high and said something Quake couldn't hear.

"Twister!" Quake called. "Guys!"

The other Weeds turned just in time to see a glittering rainbow burst from the Sparkles' scepters and stretch high into the sky. The Sparkles' feet left the branch as they rose into the colorful light.

"They're going to ride that thing!" Twister said.

"We've got to stop them! Everything you've got—
now!"

All four Weeds pointed their sticks and shouted
their most powerful spells.

Though the Sparkles had already started ascend-
ing the twinkling rainbow, their legs still dangled,
not yet inside its magical path. The Weeds used
this to their advantage. They pummeled the Sparkles' legs with burst after burst of powerful energy
blasts.

Autumn was the first to feel the tug on her ankles,
and it surprised her. The rainbow ride was always so
easy. What was wrong? Had they made a mistake
with the chant?

"It's the Weeds!" Winter shouted.

"Keep fighting it!" Summer cried. If they broke
their rainbow connection now, they'd end up locked
in battle. It was far better to escape to Mother's
realm, yet every time they lifted a little bit higher, the
swirl of Weed Power yanked them back down. The
Sparkles were the rope in a magical tug-of-war.

Autumn thought back to that morning's Sparkle

Ceremony, how she'd succeeded after a struggle. "Don't let them distract you," she said. "Concentrate on the rainbow, and how much we want to see Mother."

The Sparkles closed their eyes. Each one of them pictured Mother, and how happy they'd be to see her. Their love strengthened their magic. The glittery sparkles in the rainbow doubled, then tripled. The pull of their Sparkle Powers began to overwhelm the tug on their legs.

With a *POP*, the Sparkles suddenly shot upward into the rainbow, far faster than they'd ever soared before. Gruff shouts and wild screams followed them, which was so strange they all turned to look.

What they saw was shocking.

All four Weeds tumbled along behind them.

They were riding the rainbow too.

CHAPTER
10

Towing the Weeds up the rainbow was one thing. Towing them back down was quite another. The boys tumbled forward, crashed into the Sparkles, and at the bottom all eight of them spilled onto the ground in a jumbled heap.

"Ow!" Quake cried. "Sleet, your elbow's digging into my back!"

"That's my foot!" Summer corrected him.

"I think I have glitter in my eye," Sleet whined.

"Someone's scepter is tangled in my hair!" Twister complained.

"Sorry!" Spring said. "And ... ew."

Eventually the Sparkles and Weeds detangled from one another, but they kept their sticks and scepters poised for attack.

"Why'd you have to drag us like that?" Thunderbolt asked.

"Drag you?" Winter cried. "You tried to pull us out of the rainbow! It's not our fault you got tangled in it!"

"Why, boys!" a silky voice rang out. "How lovely of you to come for Serenity's party!"

It was Mother Nature, and the Sparkles had never been happier to hear her voice. She moved from one Weed to the next, patting their hair affectionately. "Twister, Sleet, Quake, Thunderbolt . . . I'm honored to have you in my home."

"Thank you, ma'am," Thunderbolt said quietly.

Autumn hid a smile. Faced with Mother, the boys tucked away their sticks, put their hands in their pockets, and stared down at the ground. It was like they were ashamed to be their wicked selves around Mother's incredible goodness.

"Um . . . we don't need to, um . . . stay," Twister said. "We can go back to the Barrens."

"Nonsense!" Mother Nature said. "The more the merrier! Serenity will be thrilled you want to celebrate with her. Come."

The boys dragged their feet, but none of them would dare talk back to Mother Nature. Autumn looked forward to watching them on their best behavior for the rest of the night.

Mother led them to a giant canopy of flower petals and twinkle-lights. Here the party was in full swing. Music rang out from a choir of birds and insects. They were backed by the percussive beat of trees tapping their branches together. Lions danced with antelope. Jack-o'-lanterns chatted with flamingos. Autumn even saw the vine that had startled her earlier in the day. It was curled around a monkey, and the two were dancing together. Serenity, the guest of honor, floated in the middle of everything, curled on a pillow of the whitest, fluffiest, glitteriest cloud.

"Are you ready?" Mother asked Autumn. "It's time to give Serenity her present."

Autumn's heart sank. She hated to disappoint Mother, but she'd made a mistake and it was time to be honest about it. If Mother was upset ... well, Autumn had earned that. And she'd earn it when Mother trusted her again too.

"Mother," she began, "there's something I have to tell you."

"Yes!" Summer jumped in. "Autumn had the best idea!"

"It's *wonderful*," Spring gushed.

"Autumn thought it would be really special if one of the *Weeds* gave Serenity her present," Winter said. "*Right*, Twister?"

Winter squeezed Twister's arm. He gave her a dirty look. Mother didn't seem to notice. "You know what?" she said. "That *would* be special! Thank you, Twister!"

Twister froze. "Um . . . sure. You're welcome."

Mother waited patiently. Twister looked confused.

"Serenity's present?" Mother asked.

"Yes, Twister," Winter said. "The *present*. The thing you've been *holding* for us."

"Ohhhhh!" Twister understood now, but he didn't look happy about it. He grimaced, then pulled Serenity's blanket from his pocket. Even after everything the blanket had been through, it looked just as sparkling and beautiful as the moment Autumn first saw it.

"Here." Twister shoved the blanket toward Serenity. "Happy birthday."

"It's from me, Serenity!" Mother said. "Surprise!"

She draped the blanket over her advisor, and everyone gasped. The dove and blanket complemented each other perfectly. Both were more stunning when they were together. Serenity cuddled into its coziness, then peered over her shoulders to admire it on herself. Finally she let out a series of joyful coos.

"She loves it!" Mother cried. "And she was completely surprised! Thank you, Autumn. Thank you for keeping the blanket safe."

Behind Mother, Autumn saw her sisters jump up and down and hug one another. Their plan had worked. Mother would never know Autumn made a mistake.

So why did Autumn feel so horrible?

"I lost the blanket," Autumn blurted. "It was an accident, but I used my Sparkle Powers and blew it away. If it weren't for my sisters, Serenity wouldn't have it at all. I'm not . . . I'm not as responsible as you think I am."

The last part was the hardest to say, but it was true. Autumn knew she deserved whatever she'd see in Mother's eyes, but she couldn't face it yet. She stared at the ground and waited, but Mother didn't say a word. When Autumn looked up, Mother was smiling.

"I'm proud of you, Autumn," she said.

Autumn didn't understand. "What?"

"You told me the truth," Mother said, "even though you could have gotten away with a lie. What you just did proved you *are* responsible. I love you, Autumn."

Mother wrapped Autumn in a huge hug and held her tight. When they let go, Autumn thought the whole party glistened brighter and sounded happier.

"Ready to celebrate?" Mother asked.

Autumn was, but suddenly a giant storm cloud appeared in the middle of the party. Everyone stared as it grew larger and larger, then exploded to reveal . . .

. . . Bluster Tempest!

He was tall and wore clothes so black they seemed to suck in every bit of light. His eyes were just as dark, and they flashed as he roared, "Weeds! Why did you call . . ."

His shouts faded as he looked around, confused.

"Bluster!" Mother said. "How lovely of you to join us!"

Bluster didn't seem to know how to react. "Is this a . . . party?"

"For Serenity," Mother said.

"Oh." Bluster tugged on his vest and cleared his throat. "Well. I suppose my invitation went missing?"

Mother laughed warmly and put a hand on Bluster's arm. "Bluster, of course you're invited. Have you seen the buffet? I made Hurricane Cake."

"Hurricane Cake?" Bluster asked. "Why . . . that's my favorite."

"Like I didn't know," Mother said, and led him toward the food. With Bluster no longer a threat, the music started again and everyone went back to celebrating.

Autumn looked around, taking it all in. Mother and Bluster were at the buffet together, nibbling on treats. Serenity sat on her cloud while party guests admired her sparkling blanket. Even the Weeds were busy. They had been cornered by a very friendly and *thorny* rosebush that loved to give hugs.

Autumn's sisters pulled her from her thoughts. They ran to her and pounced in a giant group hug, then pulled her into the middle of the canopy, where they whirled and twirled and danced. Autumn nearly burst with happiness, and she realized something she knew was absolutely true.

In two hundred years, she thought, *I'm going to remember this as one of the happiest days of my life.*

✳ ✳ ✳ **123** ✳ ✳ ✳

Elise Allen is the author of the young adult novel *Populazzi* and the chapter book *Anna's Icy Adventure*, based on Disney's *Frozen*. She cowrote the *New York Times* bestselling Elixir trilogy with Hilary Duff and the Autumn Falls series with Bella Thorne. A longtime collaborator with the Jim Henson Company, she's written for *Sid the Science Kid* and *Dinosaur Train*.
www.eliseallen.com

Halle Stanford, an eight-time Emmy-nominated children's television producer, is in charge of creating children's entertainment at the Jim Henson Company. She currently serves as the executive producer on the award-winning series *Sid the Science Kid*, *Dinosaur Train*, *Pajanimals*, and *Doozers*.

Paige Pooler is an artist who loves to draw pictures for girls. You can find Paige's artwork in *American Girl* magazine and the Liberty Porter, Trading Faces, and My Sister the Vampire middle grade series.
www.paigepooler.com

The Jim Henson Company has remained an established leader in family entertainment for over fifty years and is the creator of such Emmy-nominated hits as *Sid the Science Kid*, *Dinosaur Train*, *Pajanimals*, and *Fraggle Rock*. The company is currently developing the Enchanted Sisters series as an animated TV property.
www.henson.com